SKELETONS

A GUT WRENCHING TALE

WARREN BARNS
THE BARNS BROTHERS

CHAPTER 1

Jordan held a faded hand-colored photograph of a beautiful bride and her handsome groom standing in the centre of a rose garden. He'd never known his grandmother, the petite brunette in the photograph. Neither of the newlyweds was smiling, and they stood a foot apart holding hands, which was customary when posing for wedding photographs back in those days.

Jordan was the spitting image of the old man when he was younger. They both had the same big blue eyes and sandy blonde hair, with a cleft chin and slightly smaller than average ears.

He placed the photograph carefully inside a large cardboard box full of precious mementos and stood up. The sudden rush of blood to his head made him dizzy, and his back ached from sitting on his haunches for hours sorting through his grandfather's belongings.

He looked around the study, littered with books, letters, boxes, and a lifetime of accumulated junk. Jordan wondered why it was that old people's houses were always such a mess. Was he destined to one day be the same? Was it that they just stopped caring, couldn't be bothered to keep things neat and tidy, or were old people simply oblivious to the slowly growing piles of clutter that filled every surface, nook and cranny?

Jordan wiped his dusty glasses on his t-shirt, creating a large smudge across the lens. He groaned at himself in frustration. One day, when he could afford to have laser eye surgery, he would jump at the opportunity with arms wide open. Screw having to wear glasses or contact lenses for the rest of his life.

In the rush to get back home to see his grandfather before he died, he'd neglected to pack any practical items of clothing. All day long he'd been inadvertently getting dirt and cleaning products on his brand new pants without thinking, and they were going to need dry cleaning if he ever hoped to wear them on the wards again.

These weren't just any old pair of pants either; they'd cost him two weekend's worth of tips working as a waiter at a steakhouse, and he'd bought them specially for his clinical placement in the Surgical Department next semester. He sighed at himself in frustration.

Jordan's boyfriend Trevor leaned against the door jamb and gave him a smile. Despite Trevor being the child of immigrants from South Africa, he and Jordan were actually rather similar in appearance; both had a slender build, wore glasses, and on any other day would have both been dressed immaculately.

"How are you getting on?" asked Trevor.

"Oh, boy," said Jordan with an almighty sigh, "this is going to take forever to sort through. I swear Gramps hoarded everything he ever came in contact with."

He picked up a tattered old newspaper that was lying on the floor and pointed at the publication date. "April 1st, nineteen eighty-four! He's got boxes of them going back to the early seventies."

"Maybe he was a slow reader?" Trevor said sarcastically.

"Ha ha...very funny."

"Want a cup of coffee?"

"Please. I need a break."

Jordan followed Trevor down the hallway toward the kitchen. It was a grand house, with polished wooden floors, oak door frames, and high ceilings. There weren't many of these original farming homesteads left in the city. Once upon a time the grounds would have extended miles before reaching any neighboring house. Today it was surrounded by new housing developments.

"What's your family planning on doing with the house?" asked Trevor.

"Dad wants to flip it and sell, but my aunties and uncle want to keep it in the family as a rental."

Trevor ran his hands along the chipped dado rail.

"I'd personally go with what your dad said. This place is going to need so much TLC." Trevor admired a large crack in the wall. "It's going to cost tens of thousands to restore."

"I kind of like it as it is," replied Jordan. "The imperfections add character."

Jordan planned to clean out the kitchen last. It was disgusting. There were far too many jars of pickled who-knows-what sitting around the room, and a fridge that hadn't been given a wipe in years. He was sure they'd be able to culture every known family of bacteria if they took swabs of the shelves.

"Is there any pizza left over from last night?" asked Jordan. The grumbling in his tummy reminding him that it was long past lunchtime.

Trevor looked at Jordan with a guilty expression. "I ate it," he said, and cowered.

"What?" Jordan glared at Trevor.

"Sorry, babe. I was starving, and I thought we'd head out to grab something else for lunch."

"Ugh. Fine."

Trevor sidled up to Jordan. "Will you forgive me?" Slipping a hand around Jordan's lower back, he pulled him close and made the most adorable puppy-dog face.

Jordan couldn't resist Trevor's charms. He let out a

small sigh. "Fine, you can make it up to me some other way."

Trevor gave Jordan a quick kiss on the lips, then broke away to make two cups of coffee. Jordan took a seat at the dinner table and stared at the wooden surface, examining every small spiral and line of the grain.

"Hey, babe. Do you want to talk about what happened with your gramps yesterday?"

"I don't know," Jordan said rather abruptly.

"You don't know, or you don't want to talk about it?"

Trevor put two cups of steaming coffee on the table and sat next to Jordan.

"You haven't been yourself since I collected you from the hospital."

Jordan gave Trevor a dirty look. "My grandfather just died. How do you expect me to behave?"

"Okay, I'm sorry for asking. You don't need to snap at me."

Jordan looked up at Trevor. He instantly felt guilty for taking out his frustrations on the man he loved. "I'm sorry. I didn't mean to."

Trevor sipped on his coffee and waited for Jordan to continue speaking.

"I think there's a lot about my grandfather that none of us knew."

Instantly, Jordan wished he'd never said anything, but Trevor always managed to weasel these kinds of things out of him one way or another.

He took a sip from his cup and organized his thoughts, but they were interrupted by the front doorbell ringing loudly in the background. Jordan groaned. He'd had enough of his family visiting unannounced, and he had this sick feeling that one or more of them were going to be standing at the front door, no doubt hoping to come in and scavenge from his grandfather's belongings like vultures swooping for carrion.

The doorbell rang again.

"Do you want me to answer that?" asked Trevor.

Jordan stood up, scraping his chair along the wooden floorboards. "No, I'll go see who it is... and chase them away."

As he approached the front door, he saw the silhouette of two figures standing behind the rippled glass door pane.

The unwelcome guests pushed the doorbell again.

"Hold on, I'm coming," Jordan called out.

He unlatched and unlocked the front door and found two policemen standing on the steps. Twice the size of ordinary men, they were uniformed and carried large handguns at their sides.

"Good evening," said the scarier of the two policemen. "Is this the residence of Mr. Jacob Smith?"

"It is," replied Jordan. "What is this about?"

"We'd like to speak with Mr. Smith himself?"

"Of course, but you're not going to get much in the way of a response."

The policemen frowned at Jordan.

Jordan knew better than to continue being a smart ass. "He passed away two days ago."

The other policeman shook his head and mouthed "*fuck*". He turned and walked back to the police car that was parked in the driveway, grumbling to himself all the way.

"If you tell me what it was in connection with, maybe I could still help?" said Jordan.

The policeman narrowed his gaze and Jordan could sense that the man was trying to decide whether or not to waste any more time talking to him.

"What is your relationship to Mr. Smith?" asked the policeman in a rather offhand manner.

"I'm his grandson, Jordan."

"You are probably aware that a body was discovered around the corner from here, in the old Ridgemont Elementary School grounds."

"Yes, I've seen the news."

"I understand that your grandfather lived in this house for over thirty years, and that he regularly took walks through the school grounds."

"Hey may have. He did enjoy walking." asked Jordan, unsure how his grandfather's leisurely strolls through the neighborhood could possibly be relevant.

"We wanted to ask your grandfather whether he ever witnessed any suspicious activity around the school, or had cause for concern that he didn't report to the local police station."

"He never mentioned anything. Do you have any idea who it might have been?"

"I cannot comment further at this stage," the policeman said with a poker face.

"Right," said Jordan. "Is there anything else I can help you with, officer?"

The policeman smiled and shook his head. "I'll make sure to cross Mr. Smith off our list, so we don't bother you again."

"Sorry I couldn't be more help," Jordan said. "Goodnight."

"Goodnight," said the policeman. He returned to his vehicle and the two men drove down the street and parked in the neighbor's driveway.

"Who was that?" said Trevor, emerging from the shadows.

"Cops."

"What did they want?"

"To talk to Gramps."

"About?"

"A body they found buried in the school grounds."

"Oh yeah, it's been all over the news. Why would they want to speak with your gramps?"

Jordan shrugged his shoulders. "They were hoping he might have seen something suspicious."

But he wasn't being entirely honest with Trevor. Alarm bells were ringing in the back of his mind—*A body buried in the school grounds? It couldn't possibly be true!*

"I only read the headlines," said Jordan. "What did they say about it on the news?"

Trevor leaned against the wall and stretched out

his stiff neck. "They said the remains belonged to a man who died from blunt force trauma to the back of the head."

The words brought Jordan an immediate feeling of relief.

"And not just that but they think the guy died about twenty years ago."

Jordan smiled and gave Trevor a hug.

"What was that for?" Trevor asked.

"Do I need a reason?" replied Jordan with a smile.

Trevor studied Jordan's face, and stared at his boyfriend as if he were an alien.

"You all right?"

"Yeah, I'm fine."

He really did feel like a weight had been lifted off his shoulders, but he was loathe to share his thoughts with Trevor. After all, Trevor already thought he was a raging drama queen, so he kept his tumultuous inner monologue to himself.

"Okay, well, if you're hungry, I might as well start getting dinner organized so we can eat early. No more slacking off. You get back to work."

"Yes, boss," Jordan said sarcastically, and saluted.

He realized he'd been letting his own imagination run wild; it must have been a trait that ran in the family. He was grateful to have Trevor in his life to bring him back to reality when his thoughts went wandering. Sometimes, though, Trevor could be a little too pragmatic about everything and a bit of a fun vacuum. But Trevor was right, there was work to be done, and he needed to get back to it.

Trevor left to finish making dinner, and Jordan returned to the study where he'd spent most of the day. As he began packing odds and sods away in boxes, his thoughts kept drifting back to the final hours he'd spent with his grandfather. No matter how hard he tried to focus on other things, his mind just kept going back to the strange confession his gramps had made on his deathbed.

CHAPTER 2

One week earlier

Three generations of Jordan's family occupied every seat in the living room. They were in the midst of a heated discussion. Jordan's uncle was turning red in the face, and one of his aunts was threatening to cancel family Christmas this year if an agreement was not reached soon. Jordan sat in an uncomfortable antique chair in the corner of the room. He preferred to stay out of things and let his parents' generation fight things out, but as the eldest grandchild he felt a conflicting sense of duty to be present. From where he was sitting, he could see across the hallway, into the conservatory where his frail grandfather, Jacob, sat in a comfy armchair, smoking on a pipe.

He felt so sad for the old man whose life was now estimated in weeks to months. For all the time they'd spent together over the years, Jordan realized that he knew nothing of his grandfather's hopes or dreams. Did hopes and dreams belong exclusively to the younger generations, with a long life ahead of them?

It shouldn't be that way with family.

How could he know so little about someone he professed to love?

They lived in the same city for most of Jordan's life, but he could count on two hands the number of occasions where he'd spent more than a few hours at a time with Jacob. He blamed his parents. Jordan's father, Malcolm, had never had a particularly good relationship with his own father. There was always conflict between them.

When Jordan's dad met his mom, he found a new family, and although the tension between the two men settled, they might as well have been complete strangers from that moment forward.

Jordan felt it was hypocritical of his father to suddenly be so interested in managing his grandfather's affairs. None of it came from a place of kindness; his dad was a complete control freak, and Jordan could see exactly why the two men had come to blows. It made him empathize with the old man.

Jordan got up from his seat and left the room. He stopped in the doorway to the conservatory and leaned against the doorframe, taking a moment to watch his grandfather. Jacob was barely in his seventies, and yet he looked like a man decades older. He didn't look this way when Jordan left for medical school a few years before, and the drastic change in appearance was horrifying.

Jacob was so gaunt and pale.

Jordan heard his father calling his name from the living room.

"Jordan, can you come back here and give us your opinion on something," ordered Malcolm.

Every head in the living room swiveled around in Jordan's direction, and they were all staring at him.

"Sure."

"And please close the door behind you," said Malcolm, craning his neck to peer around Jordan and make sure that Jacob was still in his armchair.

Jordan headed back toward the living room, but something made him stop and take one last look at Jacob. That moment, his grandfather slumped in his armchair. The old man's smoking arm went limp, and the pipe in his hand purged its ashen contents all over the wooden floor.

"Gramps?" asked Jordan. "You all right?"

Jacob clutched at his chest. His face contorted in agony. He let out a cry that sounded more like that of a dying animal than a human being.

Jordan was the first to his grandfather's side. There was absolute chaos as family members raced to Jacob, scrambled for their phones, and paced in circles while they waited for the ambulance to arrive.

CHAPTER 3

The family members gathered around Jacob's bed. The argument had shifted to who was going to pay for the old man's medical treatment. None of them could afford private coronary care, and from what they could gather of Jacob's accounts, he was destitute, with only the house to his name.

After a war of words in the ambulance, it was decided that Jacob would be taken to the nearest community hospital. It had a shitty reputation for providing appalling medical care, but it was the most affordable option.

When Jacob first woke up, he was confused and panic-stricken. He called out for help, thinking he was strapped to an execution table, with IV lines sticking out of his veins that were slowly delivering a lethal cocktail that was going to put him to death. He finally calmed down when he realized he was in a hospital bed, an almost equally unpleasant place to wake up. It left most of Jordan's family rather distressed, and they swiftly departed en-masse.

They left not a moment too soon for Jordan's liking. It upset him that his family were all bickering and squabbling over what should be done, and in typical fashion, they somehow managed to make his grandfather's unfortunate circumstances all about themselves. He'd secretly wished for hours that they would all just fuck off.

Jordan hated being in hospital in the role of a family member. The faint odor of bleach that failed to mask the stench of looming death made him sick to his stomach. The harsh white walls hung with mass-produced prints by talentless hacks did nothing to inspire the will to live. The hospital room reminded him of a motel room, but with all the life sucked out of it.

It was all so hopelessly depressing.

Most of all, he hated the incessant noise from the machines.

Did everything in a hospital really have to make those annoying sounds? As a medical student one of the first skills he learnt was how to push the 'Silence Alarm' button. But that only brought thirty seconds of reprieve before the noise resumed. How was anyone supposed to get better with all that racket going on? *Beep...beep...blip...blip*. It was enough to drive any sane person mad.

Jordan never expected his grandfather to live

forever, however, there was something immortal inside Jacob; a cancer that had been growing insidiously over the past few years, slowly eating away at him.

"I had my suspicions," said Jacob. "Things didn't feel quite right *down there*."

"You never told anyone."

"Who would I have told? Your father?"

Jacob snorted.

"Me?"

"Oh, my boy. You're too young to remember. When your grandmother passed away from bowel cancer almost forty years ago, you couldn't imagine the devastation it wrought upon this family. Your father never got over it as a young boy. The tears, the heartache, the unanswered prayers and wasted hours negotiating with God. I didn't want any of you to go through any of that nonsense ever again."

"How did it start?"

"Do you really want to know?"

"Of course. I wouldn't have asked otherwise."

"Flecks of crimson in the toilet bowl one morning, almost exactly a year ago to the day. I thought it was nothing that a few days of hemorrhoid ointment wouldn't fix. At least that's what I tried to convince myself."

"You knew something was wrong."

"And I did nothing about it. The weight started to drop off. My clothes grew baggy, and that protuberant belly I'd struggled so hard to lose for so many years melted away without any special diet or exercise."

"Why, Gramps?"

"I didn't feel unwell. In fact, very much to the contrary. I started getting compliments from the ladies at bridge club. They usually ignored the old timers like me, and favored the younger retirees, but I loved the attention. It made me feel young again. It had been many moons since I last appreciated the soft touch and affection of a beautiful woman. I even started wondering whether I should take a giant leap and invite one of my new lady friends over for coffee... if you know what I'm saying?"

He winked at Jordan.

"You were hoping for a good old-fashioned roll in the hay. I don't blame you, Gramps."

"I dug out my treasure trove of little blue pills I'd hidden away decades ago. Even if they were past their expiry date, if the stars aligned and the opportunity arose, I wanted to be ready."

Jordan laughed. This conversation reminded him of a very similar one they'd had a few years ago when Jordan came out to his family. His father and mother had tiptoed around the gay thing, even going so far as to call Trevor his "*special friend*" for months until Jordan lost his shit and insisted they refer to Trevor as his boyfriend. Whereas his grandfather was a little more with the times, and asked Jordan if he'd discovered if he was a top or a bottom yet. Of course, he didn't actually want to know the details, and the two had burst into a fit of laughter together.

A few weeks ago, his grandfather had collapsed while walking through the park near his home. His heart attack was what ultimately led to the diagnosis of bowel cancer. That set off a flurry of family meetings and discussions behind Jacob's back about what was best for his future. But Jacob was viciously protective of his independence, and refused to enter an aged care facility, even though he knew it was probably the most sensible course of action to follow. He knew that he was incapable of caring for himself in that big old house anymore, but he wasn't prepared to give it up, not until he was well and truly at the end of his days... and Jordan respected him for it.

Light footsteps entered the room as a small girl came wandering inside ahead of her mother.

"Go give your grandfather a hug," said the woman.

"Hey, Karen," said Jordan.

"Hi, Jordan."

Karen was a bitch and by far the least loved of the in-laws. What his uncle, Dale, saw in her, God only knew, because she was a frigid ice queen who had literally no likable aspects to her personality. Jordan could only assume she had outstanding talents with her mouth or pussy that kept his uncle whipped and in line. For all her faults, she had produced one adorable little girl who everyone in the family adored.

"How's he doing?" asked Karen.

"He's lying right there, you can ask him yourself."

Karen pressed her lips tighter together. She hadn't spoken to Jacob in years, not since he'd called her out on her bullshit one Christmas Eve in front of everyone. The tantrum she threw at the time was worthy of an award.

"Maddy, go say hello to your grandfather."

Maddy ran over to Jacob's side and tugged on his index finger.

"Hey, Gramps."

His steely expression melted into a smile.

"My darling, have you come to say goodnight to Gramps?"

Maddy's mouth became downturned and her eyes watered.

She flung herself up onto the bed and wrapped her arms around Jacob's neck, holding him tightly.

"Gramps, are you sick?"

Tears flowed down her cheeks.

"No, my angel. Gramps is just old."

He tenderly hugged her tiny body close to his chest.

Karen picked Maddy up off the bed. "Come on, sweetie. Let your grandfather rest in peace."

Jordan cringed at the poor choice of words. He was certain that Karen almost smirked in self congratulation at her final "*fuck you*" remark.

Such.

A.

Bitch.

"It's okay," said Jacob. "The girl only wants to give her grandfather a hug."

"Mommy said you've got cancer, and that made Daddy upset," she whimpered and reached out for her grandfather, but her mother held on tightly. "Please don't die, Gramps."

Jacob clutched his left arm in sudden agony and let out a deep groan. Maddy squirmed out of Karen's arms and ran screaming back to Jacob's side.

"Jordan do something," yelled Karen.

Jordan's body broke out in a clammy sweat. His heart raced so fast that he thought it was surely going to explode out of his chest.

Suddenly, the room was filled with unfamiliar faces of men and women in uniforms and white coats. They pushed Jordan aside and one of the nurses led him out of the room.

It all happened so fast.

Jordan bypassed the Family Room where the rest of his relatives were gathered. The argument had progressed to what should be done about Jacob's home when the time came. It was the last thing that Jordan wanted to hear right now, so he went for a quiet walk through the park opposite the hospital.

Ten minutes later a text message appeared on Jordan's phone and he felt the vibration in his pocket. He was surprised to see that he'd missed several calls while his phone was on silent.

· · ·

— Jordan answer your phone! The doctors want to talk to us. Dad

He ran back to the hospital and raced up to his grand-father's room.

Jacob was lying on the bed with his chest covered in electrodes and more intravenous lines in both arms. He groaned and blinked his eyes.

There was a conversation going on between a man in a white coat, Jordan's father and his oldest aunt, Sally. June, the youngest, and by far his grandfather's favorite, was holding Jacob's hand. The other son, Dale, was conspicuously absent, as usual.

"Dad?" said June. "You awake?"

She squeezed his hand and smiled, a tear spilling onto her cheek.

Jacob groaned again.

"He's awake," she called out.

They all moved over to the bedside.

"I'm Dr. Broom. Can you hear me? Can you tell me your name?" said the doctor in a thick Irish accent. He spoke slowly and loudly enough that the patient in the next room would have been able to hear every word.

The old man was ill, not deaf or stupid. Jordan disliked this doctor already. Made worse by the fact Dr. Broom sounded like a leprechaun.

"Looks like he's still coming around," said Dr.

Broom. He turned to June and continued updating her on Jacob's decline.

Jordan noticed his grandfather's eyelids open ever so slightly to take a sneaky peek at his family. He caught Jacob's stare and noticed a twinkle in his eyes, so he smiled and pretended he hadn't seen a thing.

June covered her mouth to muffle a whimper. Sally stood there looking bored, and Malcolm was indifferent.

Dr. Broom continued, "This afternoon his heart went into an uncontrolled arrhythmia and he had a third heart attack."

June started choking on her tears. She was always such a drama queen.

"Anemia from his cancer probably drove the heart attack," said Dr. Broom. He paused and waited for the first bit of information to sink in. The family members stared at Dr. Broom, hanging on every word. "We've given him a couple of extra units to stabilize him, but there's now evidence of heart failure. We're trying to get the extra fluid off his lungs, but he doesn't have the best kidneys, and things aren't looking that great."

Sally's stiff upper lip faltered, and she began to cry. Malcolm lent her a comforting shoulder to cry on. They were never a close family, and it touched Jordan to see his father's generation showing solidarity, even if it was at his grandfather's expense. At least something had brought his family together for once.

CHAPTER 4

Jordan sat on an uncomfortable visitor's chair at the foot of his grandfather's bed, reading a newspaper. Sprawled across the front page was a spread of the grisly discovery of human remains found buried on the grounds of Ridgemont Elementary School. The school, which had been shut down and abandoned only a few years after his father had attended, was being torn down to make way for a new shopping mall, not that the city needed another one. Jordan hadn't paid much attention to the article.

He heard sheets ruffling and looked up to see his grandfather straining to lift himself up in bed.

"Any interesting news this morning?" asked Jacob, his throat sounding leathery and dry from snoring all night.

Jordan sprang to his feet and rushed to his grandfather's side. He raised the headrest and helped Jacob get more comfortable.

"Hey, Gramps. How are you feeling?" asked Jordan, a mix of concern and excitement on his face.

"Give this old man a hug."

The young man gave his grandfather a big bear hug, though somewhat awkwardly—there's no easy way to hug someone sprouting leads and tubes from every limb.

"You're here alone?" asked Jacob, slurring his words slightly.

"Trevor's back at the house. He wanted to give us some time alone."

Jacob stared off into the distance. Up until his grandfather's sudden turn, Jordan had been desperate for a reason to introduce Trevor to his family, but he had few opportunities to travel back home with all the demands of medical school. He'd hoped they would meet Trevor under more auspicious circumstances, Christmas or a family wedding would have been nice, but fate obviously had other plans for their introduction.

"I understand. I'm not going to be around long enough for him to get to know anyway. Better we spend this valuable time together, just the two of us. But I was hoping to meet him...my future grandson-in-law."

"Slow down, Gramps, no one's proposed just yet," said Jordan, letting out a nervous giggle. "And you did meet him...at your house a couple of days ago."

"Did I?" He seemed genuinely surprised. "Oh, I don't recall."

"The only guy in the room who had a tan? Don't you remember?"

Jacob smiled, but it was obvious that he had no idea what Jordan was talking about.

"Never mind. I'll introduce you to him again when he comes to collect me later."

"That would be nice," Jacob said with a grin. "You know your aunt June keeps me up to date with what's going on in my grandchildren's lives. Thank God, or I'd be left out of the loop completely."

Jordan raised his eyes to the heavens. "Don't believe everything she tells you. I haven't spoken with June in months."

Jacob grunted and smiled widely at Jordan.

"You shouldn't have come all this way for me. Did you boys drive or fly?"

"We drove. Trevor did most of the driving and let me sleep, but I'm sure we've already had this same conversation." Jordan paused. "I've been really worried about you."

"Oh, you needn't worry about an old man like me. Nobody else does."

"That's not true. You've got a whole family that loves and cares about you."

Jacob shifted in his bed. He clearly didn't want to talk about it.

"So where did you meet Trevor?"

Jordan realized that his grandfather was trying to

change the subject. He cringed whenever anyone asked that particular question. It wasn't as if he was going to be honest and admit to meeting Trevor on a gay dating app. So he recited the fictional—and completely believable—story that they'd dreamed up together after they officially started dating.

"Well, Trevor's in the same year as me at med school. We had Anatomy class together, and were both assigned to the same dissecting table..."

"Okay, I think I've heard enough," interrupted Jacob.

The two men chuckled.

"You know...it's the same old story. Elbows bumped, eyes flirted, one thing led to another."

"Do you have any photographs?"

"Sure. On my phone," said Jordan, reaching into his pocket. He flicked through several photos of them together, mostly embracing as a couple and socializing with friends.

"You both look very happy together," remarked Jacob.

"We are. I really think he's the one."

Jacob sighed again and smiled. Jordan tried to read his facial expressions, but he gave nothing away. Jordan's eyes travelled across the room, studying the monitoring equipment, the near empty urinary catheter bag, and charts above his grandfather's head. It all painted a rather dismal picture in his mind of Jacob's prognosis. One of the downsides of studying medicine was no longer being able to enjoy ignorance at times like these.

"I'm pleased that we'll have two doctors in the family," said Jacob. "Speaking of which, when do you graduate?"

"This year."

"Shouldn't you be at the hospital studying?"

The young man dropped his gaze. His eyes turned red and glistened with tears.

"They gave me compassionate leave, Gramps," he said with a trailing gasp.

"Oh...I see." Jacob's eyes drifted towards the window, and he stared outside at the hospital parking lot, a boring black tarmac spotted with the occasional parked vehicle.

Acid bile burnt the back of Jordan's throat. His reflux always got worse when he became anxious about something. Seeing his grandfather like this made his heart ache.

Jordan sniffed and turned away. He pulled out a tissue, blew his nose, and wiped his eyes. "Sorry, Gramps. It's hard to see you like this."

"Don't apologize. Pull your chair up closer and come sit with me."

The young man did as he was told, and sat close to the bed.

"I wish I'd got to spend more time with you over the past few years."

"Jesus, boy, I'm not gone yet!" said Jacob with an almighty laugh.

Jordan cracked a smile and laughed, too. "I didn't mean it like that."

"No. You meant it exactly the way it came out. But that's life... and all life comes to an end."

Jordan had seen many photographs of Jacob holding him as a baby, rocking Jordan's tiny wrinkled body in his big arms. Now their situations were reversed, and it was Jacob who was the vulnerable one. The order of nature, so perfectly designed to ensure that someone strong is always there to care for the weak.

Jacob's eyes flitted to the newspaper sitting on the end of the bed, and he smiled.

"Can I tell you a secret?" said Jacob, a naughty glint in his eyes.

Jordan nodded.

"You were always my favorite," he said in a whisper.

The young man patted his grandfather on the arm. "You're such a liar. I know you say that to all your grandkids."

The old man winked at him. "Nothing gets past you. That's why you're the first one in the family to enter a real profession. All my children went into information technology. So boring, staring at a computer screen all day."

"These days, almost every job involves staring at a screen."

"Pfft..." said Jacob, shaking his head. "Anyway...I'm so pleased you're here."

"Me too, Gramps. Where is everyone else? Where's Dad? I thought Aunty June, Sally, and Dad were going to be here this afternoon? "

"Oh...I sent them home. I was tired."

"Do you need me to go, too? It's almost dinner time."

"I'm not really tired. I just...you know. Family...it gets a bit much sometimes."

"That's a bit harsh, don't you think?"

"Don't pretend you don't feel the same way."

"Maybe. Mom always says I inherited all of your worst qualities."

"Does she now?" said the old man with one eyebrow arched. "You could have gone to medical school here in the city, but you chose to move one and a half thousand miles away. That was a carefully calculated move."

Jordan shrugged. His grandfather was right; he didn't feel the slightest bit guilty about uprooting himself.

"Mom was driving me insane. I had to get as far away as possible."

Jacob stared at the ceiling, lost in thought for a few moments.

"Take my advice...don't start a family. Enjoy the freedom, and don't let yourself get tied down to anyone."

"Trevor and I are actually planning to have kids someday. We just need to find ourselves an egg donor, and make us one." He scoffed as he digested his grandfather's words. "Plus...if you'd followed your own advice, *I* wouldn't be here today. "

Jacob nodded. "Good point. Still, don't have kids. Although I see your taste in men matches my taste in women. Oh, how I loved a block of smooth Dairy Milk chocolate back in the day." His eyes stared upwards as his mind drifted back to pleasant memories, an expression of blissful recollection on his face.

Jordan grimaced and closed his eyes. "How much morphine have they given you? Gran was an Irish redhead."

"You think I didn't notice? She was the love of my life. But your grandfather wasn't always a married man," he said with a big cheesy grin.

Jordan threw his hands up in defeat. "Stop. Now I don't want to know any more details."

The two men chuckled, and then there was silence. Jacob shifted in bed. Just the effort of moving left him puffing for air. He took a few deep breaths. His whole demeanor changed as he leaned to one side, facing towards Jordan.

"There is something I need to say before I go. I can feel the life slipping from this old body and I have a story to tell first."

Jordan chewed on his bottom lip. He would much rather have changed the topic of conversation. All this talk of death was making it increasingly hard to keep himself composed.

"I wasn't joking earlier. I really do have a confession to make."

Jordan gave his grandfather the evil eye. "Is it another story about pretty girls from your youth?"

"No," he said, much to Jordan's relief. "It happened when I was about eight years old."

Every ounce of excitement drained from Jacob's face and he gave Jordan a stern look.

"What is it, Gramps?"

Jacob stared down at his feet, all gloom and doom. "We all swore we'd take the secret to our graves, but I have to tell someone before I die."

"You're not going to die today, Gramps, so save your story for another time."

"No," he said, taking his grandson's hand in his.

"Okay...so what is it?"

"Not *what*...*who*, Ms. Milden," said Jacob, his heart monitor showing a sudden surge of activity.

Jordan wasn't used to his mellow grandfather acting so serious. It scared him shitless.

"Who was she?" asked Jordan, one eye watching the EKG wave dancing across the monitor behind his grandfather's head. It looked more like the output from a seismometer than a heart tracing, oscillating violently up and down.

"Take all of the worst teachers you ever had at school...wrap them up into one bundle of bitter nastiness...and you still haven't come close to describing Ms. Milden."

"But who was she?"

"One of my teachers in elementary school."

"At Ridgemont? I'm confused, Gramps. Why do

you want to talk about her? You said something about a confession? Did you steal the apple from her desk one day, or something?" He thought a joke might lighten the mood, but the old man just tittered and shook his head.

"I shouldn't have said anything," said Jacob.

Jordan backtracked. "I'm sorry. I didn't mean to make fun of you. I'm all ears. I do want to know what happened with...Ms. Milden."

Jordan sat there eagerly, just like a kid waiting for his grandfather to read him a bedtime story.

"Well," said the old man. "Where do I begin...?"

CHAPTER 5

According to legend, Ms. Milden, whose full name was Phillipa Baxter Milden, began working as a teacher at Ridgemont Elementary School back in 1862 when the school was first opened.

From a fleeting glance at her saggy eyelids and lizard-like skin, one could tell that the woman was a relic from an era long gone. A lifetime of never smiling had made her mouth turn down at the sides, and her jowls sway hypnotically whenever she talked. Her cotton candy gray hair was always tied up in a neat bun, and pulled so tight that the wrinkles were smoothed from her brow, giving her an expression of permanent surprise.

She was an evil woman, with a reputation for insisting that the children in her class adhere to a level of discipline that was near impossible to attain. She was so infamous for being strict, that every parent feared the day when the precious fruit of their loins would be in her class.

Thanks to the local council's inflexible zoned schooling system, it was an unavoidable rite of passage for every eight-year-old who lived in our leafy upmarket suburb to spend the year under her tutelage in classroom 1-D.

If a stranger were to visit her classroom on any ordinary day of the school year, they would never encounter children chewing gum, long-haired boys, unpolished shoes, or pies for lunch. She ran her classroom with military precision, and no one ever dared to disobey the rules.

Spare a kind thought for any child who scraped a chair, or spoke without being spoken to first. I always sat at the back of the classroom, near the storage cupboard. It felt safe to have that much distance between the teacher's desk and mine, but safety was an illusion.

On this particular day, from outside the classroom, no one could have guessed that twenty-eight children, the youngest only seven-and-a-half, and the oldest just about to turn nine—he was admittedly a bit slow—were sitting at their desks, working studiously, and performing well above all expectations for children their age. There wasn't a sound to be heard, not a giggle or a whisper, except maybe the dull scrape of pencil lead over paper as we worked.

Our class of angelic eight-year-olds sat in perfectly aligned rows of desks, the old kind with an ink well and lid that could open and store books and stationery inside.

Ms. Milden walked through the door with her high-heeled clogs clacking on the wooden floorboards. There was an audible gulp from the class. Everyone gripped tightly onto their chairs and curled their toes in fear. It was exactly eight o'clock in the morning, according to the clock on the wall above the blackboard.

She was always on time, never a minute late.

Milden went straight to her desk and sat herself down on her cushioned seat. She always insisted that we were to sit on the hard bare wood of our uncomfortable chairs—a numb derrière all day would, of course, help us build character.

A bunch of daisies stood wilting in a vase on the end of her desk. She snatched the flowers and tossed them into the bin, replacing them with a fresh posey that she had picked the same morning on her way to school, stolen from gardens she passed along the way.

There was a soul-destroying energy in the classroom that slowly sucked the vitality out of every living thing, the plants being no exception. She had to replace the flowers on a daily basis. It pissed her off, but each day, she persisted with a fresh, stolen, and soon-to-be-dead bouquet.

She carefully scratched her scalp with one of her talon-like fingernails, so as not to disturb the tight bun perched on her head. Then she opened the top drawer of her desk and pulled out a pair of reading glasses, which she placed on the end of her pointed and slightly crooked nose.

She was now ready for the day to begin.

A saccharine sweet smile crossed her lips.

"Good morning, class," she said in her affected English accent. The words rasped off her nodular vocal cords, damaged from a pack-a-day habit she'd enjoyed since she was old enough to tell the world to go fuck itself.

"Good morning, Ms. Milden," we replied in pseudo-enthusiastic unison.

"How are we all this morning?"

She looked around the room at our terrified faces. This was a game she loved to play. If any of us little terrors was brave enough to shout out the answer to her question without first being invited to do so, she would delight in inflicting punishment for talking out of turn.

But that day, our class was on form, and no one fell for her sly ploy.

"Good," she said. A smile crept across her thin lips. "Is anyone absent today?"

There were two empty seats. The first belonged to a wimpy girl who tragically sat one of Ms. Milden's infamous detentions all by herself earlier in the school year and was never heard from again. Several of us who sat near the back of the classroom turned and stared at the other empty seat, which belonged to Sam Lee.

"Face the front!" bellowed Milden.

Like well-trained army recruits, we faced the blackboard in one swift, uniform movement.

"I shall have a word with Sam's parents." She peered over the top of her glasses at the empty desk. "Absenteeism is simply unacceptable."

We knew the real reason why Sam wasn't there that day. After a short and painful struggle with breast cancer, his mother had passed away over the weekend. Sam's father had not attended Ridgemont Elementary as a child. He grew up on a farm a few hours north of the city, which meant that he was blissfully unaware that by keeping his son at home, he had doomed his boy to be singled out and tormented for the remainder of the school year, albeit only a few more weeks.

If poor Sam thought that his mother's death was the worst thing that was going to happen to him all year, he was in for a far more unpleasant surprise when he returned to school.

Ms. Milden opened her middle desk drawer and pulled out a crumpled wad of poster-sized sheets of paper. I could just make out the picture on top from where I was sitting; a spectacular scene of a farmyard, painted with bold brushstrokes in bright colors. I always envied the talent of the boy who'd painted it. Any parent would have been proud if their child had produced such a beautiful painting.

Milden was less than enthused.

"When I call your name, I want you to come and

collect your nauseating excuses for art," she snarled. "Ben Arnold."

She locked eyes with Ben, who sat immobile in the front row.

"Do I need to send an official invitation, Master Arnold? Move it!"

Ben stood without thinking and scraped his chair along the polished wooden floor. The children grimaced at the sound and looked at Ben with pity. He lowered his head in shame, knowing what was to come next.

Milden narrowed her gaze at the boy. He glanced up at her, expecting torrents of vile abuse to rain down upon him. Instead he was confronted by her evil stare and a finger curling, beckoning him to come forward.

Ben stepped up to the front of the class and Milden shoved his work of art into his open hands. He returned to his seat and spread the painting out across his desk, devastated at how scrunched up the paper was. As he laid it out completely, his little heart sank at the sight of a large brown coffee stain right in the center. His hard work was ruined, and he had to fight back the tears.

"Peter Fox," she called out.

Peter sat at the back of the class, a couple of desks away from me, and knew there wasn't a moment to hesitate. It took exactly five seconds to walk from his seat to Ms. Milden's desk. That was enough time for her to go from calm to cataclysmic if she thought he was dawdling. He walked briskly to the front, collected his painting, and went back to his seat, unscathed.

Mission accomplished.

"Catherine Grant."

Catherine rose carefully from her chair to avoid scraping the floorboards...so carefully that she appeared to be moving in slow-motion. Ms. Milden shook her head and heaved an exasperated sigh.

"My God, child! Could you possibly move any slower if you tried?"

Catherine, fat little cherub that she was, waddled up to the front and extended her hand to retrieve the painting from Ms. Milden. Without any warning, Milden raised a ruler high into the air, and brought it down upon Catherine's chubby palm with a giant *CRACK*! The small girl retracted her injured paw and burst into tears.

Ms. Milden stood and towered over the girl.

"What have I said about crying in my classroom? Pull yourself together or get out!"

Catherine stopped crying. She took a few short shallow breaths.

"Go sit down!"

Catherine scuttled back to her desk with her bottom lip still quivering.

"My patience has worn thin. You have all forced my hand."

She rolled the paintings up into a thick wad of papers.

"Let this be a lesson to you all for the future. I will not tolerate a lackadaisical attitude in this classroom."

She wrapped a rubber band around the bundle to hold it in place and dropped it unceremoniously into the trash can with all the other trash. The children let out a simultaneous whimper. Ben and Peter were quick to fold their creations away and hide them from view.

"If Catherine wasn't *quite* so lazy, then perhaps she wouldn't have such a fat behind, or be sprouting womanly mounds at such a tender age."

Ms. Milden closed her eyes and sighed.

I can imagine what must have been going through her mind: that she never signed up for this shit when she became a teacher, that back in her day, children knew what real discipline was and respected their elders. Cartoons, home telephones, and mothers who worked were some of the *many* things she believed were responsible for the downward trajectory of today's youth.

Her emotional temperature gauge was about to tip over from simmering point. We could tell from the engorged vein that snaked up her forehead, which acted like a mood thermometer. Right then, it was almost up to her hairline...she was pissed off.

Ms. Milden held her hand to her heart. Was it another attack of angina? She hated when that happened, and always blamed us.

Apparently, we were responsible for her bad heart. Not her smoking habit and diet of alcohol. Oh no, sir! It was our fault for putting her under so much stress.

The doctors said that her long-standing high blood pressure had weakened her heart, forcing her to take a concoction of medications every day for the rest of her life to prevent it from short-circuiting and coming to a sudden stop.

Why she felt the need to share this information with us was anybody's guess.

She hated the doctors for it, for finding her weakness, her Achilles' heel. She would proclaim from her seat at the front of the class that she'd survived two Great Wars and wasn't going to let a problem with electrical conductivity stop her, even if she had to put her fingers in a power socket to jumpstart her own heart.

Every day, we wished she'd follow through with her threat.

"Now, everyone," said Ms. Milden in her calmest tone of voice, "I want you to take out the assignment that you were asked to complete for homework last night."

We opened our desks and quickly rummaged to find our homework books. We put the desk lids down quietly and folded our arms in front of us; all except Johnny Walters. He was a hopeless case. He would arrive at school fully dressed and return home with two left shoes and his underwear gone astray. He truly was that legendary boy who was so absent-minded that he would lose his own head if it weren't connected to his body.

Johnny scratched madly through his desk in search of his homework. From his mumbling, he seemed certain that he'd brought it in with him today. He may have been a scatterbrain, but he wasn't stupid. You'd have to be a raging lunatic, or a complete imbecile, to deliberately not do as told by Ms. Milden.

"Come on, please be here. You've got to be here," whispered Johnny to himself, his fear clearly growing with each passing second, as did ours for his safety.

Ms. Milden loomed ominously over him. He silently closed the lid of his desk and nearly shit in his pants

"I see that *somebody* has neglected to do his homework," she said.

Johnny shook his head. "No, Ms. Milden. I promise I did it. I...I must have forgotten it at home," he said in desperation.

Milden ignored his pleas and continued her tirade.

"What happens, *Johnny*, when a pupil in this class fails to do his or her homework?"

"But I did it," he whined. He whipped out his homework notebook and pointed at his mother's signature beside yesterday's date.

She yanked his head back by his blond curls. Johnny yelped in pain as his scalp stung from the hair being ripped at the roots. Ms. Milden made no attempt to hide the look of delight on her face as she raised her hand high above her head. Johnny closed his eyes and braced himself.

With an open palm, she swung at his rosy cheek.

Then all of a sudden, midway through the arc of her blow, she froze, and the color drained from her face. She pummeled her chest with a closed fist, and wheezed like a dying dragon that had run out of flame.

Johnny cracked open an eyelid and breathed a sigh of relief as Ms. Milden stumbled back to her desk.

"My pills! I need a pill. My heart..." she gasped, taking huge gulps of air like a fish dying on dry land. "You see what happens...when you make me mad. My poor...pounding heart!"

She reached up and snatched the bottle of pills that always sat on the corner of her desk. She tipped a couple out, and tossed them into her mouth. We knew from one of her previous oversharing rants that her doctor had given explicit instructions to place the pills under her tongue and let them dissolve, but as her eyeballs travelled in different directions and glazed over, that was probably the last thing on her mind. I imagined the pills bouncing off her tongue and hitting the tonsils hard, ricocheting off her uvula and shooting into her gullet.

Then she began to choke. The pills hadn't gone down; they were lodged in her throat. We looked on in absolute horror, but remained glued to our chairs. Had her time finally come, or was she merely flirting with death? I wanted to look away, but it was like watching the spinning prize wheel on the State Lottery. Was it going to be our lucky day, or was there a booby prize lined up in our immediate future?

Ms. Milden clutched at her neck and tried to milk the pill down, but it did her no good. She grabbed the vase off her desk and brought it to her lips. Those with a flair for the dramatic retched in disgust as she gulped mouthfuls of the putrid flower water, rinsing the pills down her dry throat.

Ms. Milden heaved several deep breaths, and the color returned to her cheeks.

No, we had not won the lottery that day. The pain had subsided, and now she was itching for a fight.

"That's better," she said, giving Johnny a twisted smile. "Just a little angina. Nothing to be concerned about."

She wasn't finished with him yet.

Johnny's little face began to crumple, and tears pooled in the corners of his eyes.

"I'm sorry, Ms. Milden," he said in a timid voice, his eyes cast down at the floor.

"Speak up, boy! I can't hear you," she bellowed across the room.

"I'm sorry, Ms. Milden," he said, his voice full of desperation. "It was a mistake to make you so mad."

She stormed over to his seat and grabbed Johnny by the ear. She twisted his earlobe and hauled him to the front of the class. He screamed and dragged his feet, but resistance was futile.

"You hurt me; now I'm going to hurt you, Johnny," she said and pinched his cheek painfully hard. "It's children like you, Master Walters, who will one day go on to destroy the foundations of our great society. Today you ignore your homework; tomorrow you're binge drinking yourself sick, snorting cocaine off hookers' breasts, and impregnating sluts all over town. I cannot abide this kind of degeneration. We're on the brink of a moral collapse. Rules exist for a reason. I blame your parents. I could see it coming when they were sitting in these very same seats in front of me. They were almost as bad as you lot. No wonder you're all growing up to be such little shits!"

"Mmmo—" Johnny began to wail.

"Mmmo...what?"

"I want my mommy," he squeaked.

Milden released her pincer grip on his earlobe and dropped to her knees beside him. The sad expression on her face could have been mistaken for genuine remorse. Johnny flinched and edged away from her.

"Does little Johnny want his mommy?"

The fake sympathy vanished, and the vein in her forehead bulged again as her blood finally reached boiling point. "That is the single most pathetic thing I have ever heard in my entire life. Harden up, you runt!"

She marched to the back of the room, dragging Johnny alongside her, and wrenched the doors open of a tall wooden cupboard. Inside was a shovel, a pair of rubber gloves, rope, a hockey stick, a tennis racket —the list went on. She picked up the shovel and looked at it quizzically.

"Where did this come from?" she said quietly under her breath, putting the shovel back in its place.

She played a game of internal *eeny, meeny, miny, moe*, her index finger hovering over each potential implement of torture, before settling on the tennis racket. It was her weapon of choice for doling out pain because the holes in the strings meant less air resistance, and a more satisfying swing.

A shadowy figure appeared in the doorway and cleared his throat. Ms. Milden shut the cupboard door and spun around to see who was standing there. It was Principal Harvey, one-time champion jockey, in all his five feet and two inches of unimposing glory. With his boyish looks and tiny stature, he could easily have been confused for one of the students. He folded his arms and leaned against the doorframe.

Ms. Milden's manner changed completely. Her body language softened, and she stroked Johnny's head as if he were a pet. It reminded me of how my mom would behave some evenings when Dad came home from work, shortly before I was ordered to bed early and my parents' bedroom door was shut for the night. Back then, I wasn't fully up to speed on the birds and the bees.

"Principal Harvey, I didn't see you standing there," said Ms. Milden with a coquettish smile and flutter of her eyes.

In hindsight, it was impossible to deny the obvious signals between Ms. Milden and the principal. They undoubtedly had more than just a working relationship.

"Could I please have a word with you in my office?" Principal Harvey asked in an oddly high-pitched voice. "There is something we need to discuss."

Milden nodded like a giddy schoolgirl. Principal Harvey flashed her a devilish grin and a sexy wink before disappearing down the corridor.

Ms. Milden twirled around to face our class. "Children, would you excuse me for half an hour? Continue with the work I set for you this morning."

She gave Johnny a gentle shove, and he skedaddled back to his seat, a lucky escape.

Milden opened her bottom desk drawer and took out a girdle, whip, and handcuffs. She hesitated for half a second, then placed the handcuffs back in the drawer. "Another time," she said to herself. She looked up to address the class. "I'll be back in exactly half an hour. And don't let me catch any of you talking!"

A trembling hand, belonging to Cindy Miller, rose into the air. Ms. Milden shot Cindy a look that must have scared a few years off the girl's life.

"What, Cindy?" she spat.

"B-b-b-but, Ms. Milden. I f-f-f-finished my w-w-work from this morning already," stuttered Cindy.

I wanted to throw something at Cindy, but it

would have only transferred the focus from Little Miss Suck-Up to me. Ms. Milden chuckled and walked over to the mighty bookshelf that spanned the length of the classroom. She scanned the spines of the books until her finger came upon the title she was searching for.

She pulled the textbook out and walked over to the blackboard. She plucked up a piece of chalk and wrote out "*High School Calculus, pages 115 to 123*". We sank in our chairs in despair. A few of my classmates threw nasty looks at Cindy for adding to our misery. No one likes an overachiever at the best of times.

"That should keep you all sufficiently occupied until my return," she said with an evil grin.

As a bright idea popped into her head, Ms. Milden stopped just short of the door.

"I would also like to inform you that due to your classmate's poor work ethic, you will all be sitting my detention...tonight...from seven until midnight. Do I hear any objections?" she asked.

There was a deafening silence. Ms. Milden marched off, twirling the whip in one hand and clutching the girdle in the other.

What kind of teacher makes her class sit detention on a school night, long after they should be tucked up in bed? Milden knew that none of our parents would complain. They never did. It was almost like a game to her, seeing how far she could push the limits. But no challenger had ever stepped up to the plate. They were all too terrified, even long after they had graduated school and grown up. She left her mark on our parents' psyches, and like tortured animals that had been experimented on by sadistic scientists, they cowered in fear at the mere thought of her.

We were on our own, and would have to fend for ourselves.

And fend for ourselves we did.

CHAPTER 6

Jacob went very still, and his eyes drifted closed.

"Gramps, are you okay?"

Jordan eyeballed the monitoring equipment. A surge of adrenaline rushed through his veins as the EKG wave flatlined. Several alarms blared at once.

Don't panic, the young man thought to himself. *You know what to do.*

He hit the emergency button on the wall behind his grandfather's head. He ran on instinct and automatically went through the ABCs he'd been taught at med school. He tilted the old man's chin up to open his airway and put an ear to his grandfather's face. He couldn't hear or feel any breath on his cheek. Jordan climbed up onto the bed beside his grandfather. He started chest compressions.

One, two, three...all the way to thirty. He checked for breathing, but could hear nothing.

"Step aside. We'll take it from here," said one of the crash team nurses in a loud, authoritative voice.

Jordan hadn't even noticed the small team of nurses and doctors who'd entered the room behind him. Before his feet touched the floor, the nurse had opened up his grandfather's hospital gown and applied electrodes to his chest.

"Stand clear," said another nurse who was manning the defibrillator.

Everybody stepped back, and she hit the big red button.

The old man's body spasmed, and his back arched dramatically. His eyes sprung open, and he sucked in air like a blocked vacuum cleaner that had come unstuck. Jordan watched, frustrated that he could do nothing more to help. The nurse injected several drugs into the IV line and stood back. Within seconds, his grandfather's heart rhythm returned to a stable, yet irregular beat. The nurses fussed over the old man to make him comfortable and relaxed.

Jordan felt a pat on the back.

"Well done," said one of the doctors who had been watching from the sidelines. Jordan was at a loss for words, and replied with a glimmer of a smile. "Although your grandfather was DNR." He frowned at Jordan as he left the room.

Dr. Broom appeared beside Jordan.

"Can I have a quick word?"

"Sure."

Dr. Broom led him to the farthest corner of this tiny room. He huffed, and chose his next words carefully. "He isn't looking good—"

No shit, thought the young man, but decided it was best to keep the opinion to himself.

"We've been giving your grandfather an inotrope to keep his heart pumping."

"Doesn't look like it's working," Jordan interjected.

"No, it was," said the doctor, "but we stopped the infusion an hour ago."

"Why would you do that?" Jordan asked in disbelief. "Who agreed to that?"

"Your grandfather did. Look, we can't keep giving it to him forever. He's on borrowed time and it's only going to delay the inevitable. And if he has another crash like this...well..." The doctor glanced at Jacob and shrugged.

"What are our options?"

Jacob croaked as loudly as he could from his bed, "I think I'd like to be a part of this conversation."

"Sorry, Gramps. Did you hear what the doctor said?"

"I don't want any drug that is going to keep me alive longer than God intended. Do you hear me?" he said sternly.

Jordan was shocked by the statement. He'd experienced similar situations with patients during his training, but to hear it from his own family member made his blood run cold.

"I'm going home, but one of my colleagues will be through to see you later this evening. In the meantime, we'll do everything we can to make you comfortable." The doctor smiled fleetingly, then went on his way.

The old man waved him off with a middle finger.

"What a jerk," muttered Jacob.

The last of the nurses in the room offered Jacob a sip of water from a straw cup. Jordan caught a glance at her name badge, *Rebecca*, and gave her a smile.

"Is there anyone you'd like me to call?" asked Rebecca.

She gently brushed a hand over Jacob's shoulder. It was a simple gesture, but showed how much she truly cared about her patients. Jordan was paying careful attention. He thought the doctors treating his grandfather could learn a thing or two from her.

"My dear," replied the old man, "I don't want to take any time away from your more important tasks."

"You just let me know if you need anything," she replied. She looked over at Jordan. "Anything at all, just ring the bell."

He thanked her with a smile, and she walked out. It was once again just the two of them.

"Scared you, didn't I?" chuckled Jacob.

"You have no idea. I thought that was it."

"I almost didn't get to finish telling my story. I was just getting to the good part." He winked at Jordan.

"I thought *my* teachers were horrible. Ms. Milden

sounds like she worked for the Gestapo in a previous life."

"Oh, don't you worry. She got what she deserved," said Jacob, coldly.

Jordan was intrigued. He cocked his head to one side. "What happened to her?"

"I just need to rest my eyes for a few minutes, and then I'll tell you some more."

CHAPTER 7

Ms. Milden's detention wasn't like any ordinary detention. It always began with some form of physical punishment, for no other reason than because she could. That evening, she had chosen a particularly cruel warm-up event—the wall sit. She made us take turns, five at a time, lined up against the wall while the rest watched and waited their turn.

We were ordered to stand with our backs against the wall with our feet shoulder-width apart, then slowly lower our hips until our knees formed a perfect right-angle. We were instructed to stretch our arms out in front of us, with palms facing down. If any of us so much as quaked at the knee, we would instantly receive a blow to our outstretched hands from Ms. Milden's metal ruler.

Only when all five children had assumed the position did the countdown begin. Five minutes of the most excruciating pain imaginable, burning through our thigh muscles. Five minutes of pure hell.

"Look at those filthy fingernails!" she declared as the first five victims lined up against the wall. "Absolutely disgusting! Where is your basic hygiene?"

Like criminals forced to stand before a firing squad, they shivered and shook, sweat pouring down their foreheads. Sweet Catherine was one of them. Her Coke-bottle legs didn't stand a chance of supporting her hefty bulk. She knew that there was no hope for her. Stinging knuckles had a guaranteed place in her very near future. But still, she fought against the pain and the burn. Her legs wobbled and shook, but her concentration remained steadfast.

Milden stood over Catherine with the ruler tucked behind her back, ready to deliver a single, sharp blow. But something extraordinary happened. Catherine trembled—she may have even farted a little—but she never quaked, and her knees remained locked at ninety-degrees.

We all counted down the last thirty-seconds—in our heads, of course, we weren't stupid—and when the clock reached five minutes, and all five children had passed the seemingly impossible task, Ms. Milden calmly lay down her ruler and motioned for them to return to their desks.

The next five lined up in single file against the wall, but they were no longer fearful. We all knew that if fat Catherine could make it through this punishment and get out on the other side unharmed, the rest of us could too.

Alas, our proclaimed victory was premature. At exactly two minutes and twenty-two seconds in, the first one caved.

It was Ben.

Smack!

Two of the others flinched so hard from the sharp sound of metal cracking on skin that they, too, lost their footing and slipped.

Smack! Smack!

There were no yelps or cries of pain. They gritted their teeth and blinked the tears away. Showing any sign of weakness would only lead to further discipline.

Milden sent all five back to their desks and called up the next group. This continued until every child had their turn, including me. Fortunately, I weighed so little back then that I practically levitated against the wall.

In total, six unfortunate souls were left nursing stinging knuckles that night. Ms. Milden was somewhat dissatisfied with the result. Our class was far more resilient than the "*Sniveling batch of wimps she had last year.*"

Her words, not mine.

After the wall-sits were over and yet another impossibly difficult task had been set from a textbook far above the expected intellectual capacity for children our age, we were finally able to relax and enjoyed a reprieve.

Ms. Milden reclined in her chair and opened her erotic romance novel, hoping to continue the story where she left off, right at the point where the heroine was about to engage in carnal delights with another sexy minx to entertain the hero. We knew this because Jessica, who sat right in front of Ms. Milden, could read text fluently upside-down, and loved to regale us with sexy lines that she had memorized.

I imagined that purple prose was one of Ms. Milden's simple pleasures, one of the few things in her life that still got the blood coursing through her stiff veins. She had just found her spot on the page, when her bat-like ears detected a muffled whisper.

She peered over her reading glasses and scanned the rows of desks. Like a human lie-detector, she eyed each of us in turn, searching for any signs of guilt. We knew better than to look anywhere other than directly into her hollow eyes. Her radar was never wrong. She knew exactly who had shattered the silence and broken her concentration, but she wanted the culprit to demonstrate honesty in the face of adversity—or in simpler terms, she wanted him to squirm.

"Did I hear a whisper?

The question was aimed at no one in particular.

Peter sank in his chair and swallowed hard on the lump that had formed in his throat. I could tell that he knew he'd messed up in the split-second that it took for the air to rush from his lungs and tickle his vocal cords, but he couldn't help it. He was one of those people who worked through difficult maths problems by verbalizing his steps. It was a strategy that worked well for him, and he was one of the few children who had actually excelled at whatever Ms. Milden had thrown our way this year.

Ms. Milden daintily closed her book and placed it on her desk. She rose to her feet and clenched her fists, her knuckles cracking.

"I am only going to ask one more time. Who whispered?" she said in a vicious staccato.

Below the desk, Peter's legs started to shake uncontrollably. He used all his inner strength to maintain his composure from the waist up. I'm sure what he really wanted to do was scream and run from the room crying.

"I know who spoke. You may as well confess and face your punishment. The alternative is far worse."

Peter never even blinked.

"Very well. I shall pick three of you at random, and you will be punished in lieu of your classmate."

We breathed a collective gasp. It was an unfair punishment, even by Ms. Milden's ruthless standards. Milden wallowed in the fresh terror that she had drawn out of our class. She pointed her arthritic claw at Andy, who sat across the aisle from Peter; Sarah, whose seat was beside Peter's; and Joanne, who sat directly in front of Peter. If the boy was under any illusion that he had not been identified as the perpetrator, Ms. Milden's selection of students made it abundantly clear that she knew it was he who had spoken.

"Stand up." She flicked her hands towards the ceiling.

From the look on Sarah's face, I knew she was tossing up whether or not to end her own misery and throw Peter under the bus. She wasn't his biggest fan at the best of times, and had so far managed to avoid any major interaction with Ms. Milden as a consequence of her small stature and desk location at the rear of the classroom. She bit hard on her tongue and stood up tall. Joanne and Andy did the same, though Andy looked like he was about to cry. Joanne's hands were clasped behind her back so tightly they were turning red and blue in places.

"Come to the front," ordered Ms. Milden, staring impatiently at the ceiling.

Sarah dug her fist into Peter's spine as she walked past his desk. Peter winced in pain from the surprise attack. He almost shouted out "ouch", but bit his tongue and tried not to screw up his face.

Moments later, Ms. Milden lowered her gaze. The three innocent parties marched slowly towards their doom.

"Stand in a triangle. Come on, quickly now," she said, directing the three to form a triangle at the front of the class. "Hold out your right hand, about a ruler's length from the face of the person standing to your right."

The three children complied with the peculiar

command, giving a sideways glance to the hand that was now hovering beside their left cheek.

"The rules of this game are simple: I will give you three a mathematical problem to solve; if you know the answer, yell 'bang'. If you get the answer correct, then you will be allowed to return to your desk; if your answer is incorrect, then I will call out 'wrong', and the person whose hand is closest to your face will bring their open palm swiftly to your cheek."

I felt a swarm of butterflies take flight in my stomach. How could Peter be such a coward? How could he sit there and watch Sarah, Joanne, and Andy slap each other in the face on account of his foolish mistake? Peter appeared to have succumbed to terror and all he could do was sit in stupefied silence.

"First question," Ms. Milden said smugly. "There are two planes. One is flying from New York to London at a speed of five hundred miles per hour. The other is flying from London to New York at a speed of four hundred miles per hour. When the two planes meet, which one will be closer to London?"

"Bang!" shouted Andy, bubbling with pride. He must have assumed that his instincts were right, that he knew the answer. It was so simple, after all. "The plane flying from London...because it's going slower."

Sarah's head drooped in utter despair of her dimwitted friend.

Joanne's bottom lip quivered.

Andy stood tall and proud.

There was a twinkle in Ms. Milden's eye. "Wrong."

Ms. Milden looked at Sarah, her piercing stare daring the girl not to follow through with doling out Andy's punishment.

Peter squirmed in his chair. I knew that he was fond of Andy. They weren't the greatest friends, but they played sports together and seemed to enjoy each other's company.

"I *said* 'wrong'," repeated Ms. Milden in a cool monotone.

Through facial expressions alone, Andy pleaded with Sarah to be gentle. She dipped her head slightly to nod that she understood.

Slap! The sound of skin smacking against skin made everyone in the room cringe, all but our tormentor. Tears flooded Andy's eyes and rolled down his cheeks, but he stood stoic. He didn't want to give Ms. Milden the pleasure of seeing him crumble.

"Andy, you may sit down," said Ms. Milden.

Andy didn't need to be told twice. He scuttled back to his seat, glaring daggers at Peter.

Peter started to take long deep breaths, with a barely audible wheeze.

"The answer," continued Ms. Milden, "is that both planes are the same distance from London when they meet. Imbecile."

The two girls were left at the front of the class, standing opposite each other, hands outstretched and ready to swat the other's cheek.

Ms. Milden began to pace from the door to her desk, and back again.

"The next round is a lightning round. Instead of calling out 'bang', you will strike your opponent. Whoever lands the first blow gets to answer the question. The same rules from the first round apply if you get the answer wrong."

Joanne explained to me later how she mentally rehearsed what she was about to do. She tried to tell herself that it was nothing personal; either she hit Sarah, or Sarah hit her. She furrowed her brow.

Sarah stone-cold stared back into Joanne's eyes, lower eyelids twitching from nervous anticipation.

"A boy is twice as old as his sister, and half as old as their father. In fifty years, his sister will be half as old as their father. How old is the boy now?"

I couldn't stand to see any more of what was going on. How could Peter sit there and watch while his classmates—his friends—were forced to assault one another?

Then something incredible happened. Peter rose to his feet, knocking his chair back so it fell flat on the floor. Every head turned to look in his direction, including Ms. Milden's. No child had ever been so defiant.

It was then that I realized—this is it, *this* is the moment we've been waiting for.

"Peter Fox!" boomed Ms. Milden.

"Stop it!" shouted Peter. "I won't let you hurt them."

Sarah gave Peter a flickering smile.

"Oh, will you now? And how are you going to accomplish this mighty feat?"

Ms. Milden stalked Peter like a lioness about to make her kill, slowly edging closer to his desk at the back of the classroom.

"A sniveling little worm like you?"

Peter took another step forward. "I'm warning you, Ms. Milden. If you hurt her..." his words trailed off, and he shook his finger at her.

The two of them met halfway down the aisle, monster and mouse.

"How dare you! You impudent child!" She slapped him across the face. "How dare you disrespect me!"

Peter's head was knocked to one side, but he straightened himself up again. His cheek flushed red, and a handprint began to form.

"You'll regret that," he said.

Milden snickered, but only for a second, before Peter's fist caught her in the gut. He charged at her with all the force he could muster, and shoulder-barged her into the air. She flew backwards and landed on her bony backside on the floor, sliding past three rows of desks.

Peter stood over her and bellowed. "Don't you *ever* do that to another child! Do you hear me?"

Milden gasped, heaved, choked, and started to turn blue in the face. She held her chest and dragged herself along the floor towards her desk. She clutched onto the side of her desk and drew herself up. Her hands flailed about, searching for the bottle of pills that contained her heart medication. All the while, we remained seated at our desks, shifting anxiously, and perfectly quiet.

"My pills," gagged Ms. Milden.

She locked eyes with each of us, her expression begging someone, anyone, to come to her aid. Her eyes turned glassy and rolled back in their sockets. Her body slumped against one of the desk legs, the force toppling the vase, spilling what was left of its putrefying contents over her head, and sending the bottle of pills rolling over the edge of the desk and into her open hands.

The cold water roused Ms. Milden. She used the last of her strength to turn the bottle cap, nostrils flaring as she looked out at the class with victory in her eyes, triumphantly mocking every one of us.

She tipped the bottle over...and nothing came out.

"You little shits," were the last words to escape her lips.

The whole class rose from our seats, and a quiet murmur spread around the room. Johnny and Ben were the first to reach the body.

"Is she dead?" asked Cindy.

Johnny tapped Ms. Milden's leg with his shoe.

"I think so," said Johnny.

Sarah gave Peter a hug. The poor guy was tremulous with fear, and had a wet spot in the front of his pants.

The class surrounded Ms. Milden. We stared at

her corpse in disbelief. She looked so peaceful, like a sweet only granny.

"I can't believe she's dead," said Catherine, feeding her fat little face with a chocolate bar.

"You lot need to quit standing around and get the shovel," said a squeaky voice from a boy sitting at the desk nearest to the door. Everyone was surprised to hear Mark talk. He pushed his oversized glasses up his nose. "We've still got a few feet to dig before we can bury the body."

The wooden floor creaked under their feet and all eyes looked down.

"Why can't we just put her under the floor-boards?" said Catherine. "Our parents will be here to pick us up in an hour."

"She has to be six feet under...or they'll smell her," said Mark matter-of-factly.

Catherine turned her nose up in disgust.

Ben pried the empty bottle from Ms. Milden's hands. She was exceptionally stiff for a body so recently deceased. He opened his desk lid and looked inside at a handful of pills scattered over his books. He plucked up each pill individually and put it back inside the bottle before placing it on the desk where it belonged.

"Did you put them all back?" asked Cindy.

"All fifteen pills," said Ben with a smile.

"Somebody fetch the shovel," ordered Cindy.

Just as suddenly as the uprising began, our coup was now complete.

CHAPTER 8

J ordan stared at the shiny white floor tiles, a look of bewilderment on his face. He turned to Jacob and screwed up his face, about to ask a question, when a nurse he'd never met before entered the room. She too had a look of grave concern on her face.

"Excuse me," said the nurse. "The doctor has asked if he could speak with your grandfather."

"Oh, sure," said Jordan, rising from his seat.

Jacob grabbed hold of Jordan's wrist. His grip was weak, but forceful.

"No, stay," said Jacob.

The nurse smiled and said, "The doctor will be through shortly." Then left the room.

"You're the only person I know who speaks their language. This medicine talk is all mumbo jumbo to me. I may need you to act as an interpreter."

A doctor marched into the room, another unfamiliar face. He was a young man in his mid thirties, with his hair slicked back and wearing a stylish suit. He reeked of Armani and arrogance. He gave the grandson a disdainful look before picking up the medical chart.

"And how are we feeling this evening," the doctor said in a patronizing tone, still not making any eye contact with his patient, or even sharing his own name.

"*We* are feeling like shit," said Jacob.

"Hmm...to be expected," replied the doctor, like a well-trained robot.

Rebecca, the sweet nurse who had been taking care of his grandfather earlier in the day, slipped quietly into the room and stood in the corner.

"Has he had all his meds today?" asked the doctor to no one in particular.

"Yes, doctor," Rebecca said in a servile manner.

"Including his risperidone?"

Jordan recognized the drug name, but searching through his memory of clinical pharmacology classes he came up blank. He'd have to look up the drug when he got back home.

"Yes. He's had everything that was charted."

"Good."

The doctor unceremoniously took Jacob's wrist and felt for a pulse, staring into the distance. He then proceeded to shove his fingers into the old man's neck and time the pulse on his watch.

"Hmm," muttered the doctor. "Pulse is weak and irregular." He shook his head gently. "Not good."

"The man has a talent for pointing out the obvious," said Jacob with a chuckle.

The doctor didn't see the funny side, and stared blankly at the two men.

"Unfortunately, I don't have good news. I'm going to be brutally honest with you. The only reason you're still with us is because of the drugs we're giving you to keep your heart beating. I'm sorry...but we have two options in the coming days that you need to consider. We can stop treatment altogether, in which case you will probably die in a few hours from a failing heart; or we can keep you alive with medications, and the cancer will take you in a few weeks, or, if you're lucky, months' time. There are exciting, but very costly immune therapies now available to treat these cancers, but you're unlikely to be a candidate given your poor performance status."

The doctor sighed, showing the first sign of having any emotions, or perhaps it was impatience. Jordan shook his head in despair at the worst example of breaking bad news he'd ever witnessed in his short medical career.

"Then what happens?" asked Jacob. He looked at his grandson whose eyes were welling with tears. "Is there a third option? I'd probably like to take that one."

"I'm sorry," said the doctor. "I think it's time for us to call your family and tell them to come in."

Jordan already knew things were progressing from bad to worse, but that didn't make it any easier to hear.

"Thank you, doctor," said Jacob. "By the way, what was your name?"

"I'm Dr. Singh."

"Pleasure to meet you, sir," said the old man, much to his grandson's disgust.

The doctor nodded at Jacob and Jordan, then left the room.

"That guy was a total asshole," said Jordan.

"Let that be a lesson to you on how *not* to treat your own patients someday."

Jordan raised his eyebrows and nodded, but it wasn't the first time he'd seen doctors behave like that. His entire first year on the wards was spent learning from the experts how *not* to be a good doctor.

"You look tired, Gramps," remarked Jordan.

It was an understatement. Jacob looked like death warmed up. There was an insidious drowsiness creeping over him that wasn't simply exhaustion.

The young man exhaled deeply and shook his head. He scratched his forehead and searched his grandfather's face for answers.

"You're making this up, right?" asked Jordan. "This story about Ms. Milden. One last joke to make up for all the April Fools' Days we'll never share again."

The old man stared at him, unflinching.

Jordan pushed himself to his feet. He paced

around the foot of the bed. "So you're telling me this story is true?"

"We made a pact to take the secret to our graves... assuming no one found out before then. But I couldn't, and I'm the last to go."

Jordan stood there, uncertain what to say.

"Please don't think any less of me," said Jacob.

"I don't know what to think, except maybe you've had a bit too much morphine today."

Jacob chuckled, and then there was a silence between them. He had several false starts at continuing the conversation, something on the tip of his tongue, but each time, he withdrew back into his own thoughts.

"Tell me what happened after that. After you'd buried the body," said Jordan.

Jacob gave him a wry smile and continued with the tale.

CHAPTER 9

Mark, who sat closest to the door, stood on his chair and kept watch through the small window that looked down into the corridor outside, giving us a running commentary of everything he could see.

We were gathered by the door, listening to the echoed conversation taking place between Principal Harvey and two policemen. Harvey was a pitiful, blubbering mess of tears and snot. The two policemen, Lieutenant Royce and Sergeant Harry, who could have been twins, both with bulging bellies, pedophile mustaches—which were popular at the time—and receding hairlines, were asking him questions about Ms. Milden's sudden disappearance.

"I told you," sniffled Principal Harvey. "She was here one day and gone the next. I haven't seen her in over a week."

"And the two of you had a good working relationship?" asked Royce.

"She is irreplaceable," bawled the principal.

Lieutenant Harry was losing patience, the frustration written all over his face. Principal Harvey was clearly full of shit and wasn't going to be much help with solving this case.

"We should talk to the kids," said Harry.

Royce nodded and put the notepad that he'd been scribbling on back into his pocket. "This her classroom?" Harry pointed at classroom 1-D, and caught Mark staring at him through the window.

Sergeant Harry winked, and Mark ducked down.

"Hurry," said Mark. "They're coming!"

We scrambled for our seats. The policemen, and our diminutive principal, were on their way.

The classroom looked very different than it did only a week before. Our artwork adorned the walls, thriving flowers that were almost a week old stood in the vase on Ms. Milden's desk, and we'd arranged the desks in groups around the classroom so we could sit with our friends. We pretended to read at our desks like good pupils as the three adults walked through the door.

"Children," said Principal Harvey in a meek voice. "Please say good morning to Lieutenant Royce and Sergeant Harry."

The children stood up, chairs scraping across the wooden floor. Ms. Milden would have been turning in her grave. "Good morning, sirs," we chanted out in chorus.

"Where's the substitute teacher?" asked Royce.

"I haven't been able to bring myself to call in a substitute. They're so well behaved, anyhow. A testament to the fine work that Phillipa did...does." The principal's voice broke. He cleared his throat. "Children, you might see the two policemen around the school over the next few days. They'll be protecting the innocent and making our school grounds a safer place for everyone." He swung his arms with gusto, but his delivery fell flat.

"Kids, we're actually here on more serious business," said Harry rather bluntly. "Have any of you seen Ms. Milden?"

None of us dared to blink an eyelid. But Cindy knew what she had to do. If it came from her, it would seem more plausible. She was the biggest suck up in the class, after all. She raised her hand high in the air.

"No need to put up your hands. Yes, little girl," said Harry.

"My name is Cindy, sir," she corrected him.

Mark, who was sitting behind the policemen, glared at Cindy. This was no time for her to deviate from what they'd practiced to perfection umpteen times over the last week.

"When is Ms. Milden coming back?" asked Cindy, curling her bottom lip and feigning dejection.

Principal Harvey burst into tears.

"We'll take it from here, Principal Harvey. You can

go now," said Royce, ushering out the diminutive man, who appeared to be getting on the police officer's last nerve.

Harry followed Royce and Harvey back out into the corridor. Mark perched up against the windowsill and watched as the principal pulled out a cigarette and started smoking.

"It's just that I can't understand what happened," said Principal Harvey, drawing in a huge breath of cancerous fumes.

"We've been to her house. It was like a museum," said Harry.

"A museum with cats everywhere," sniggered Royce.

"Husband couldn't tell us much. He'd starved to death by the time we figured out where she lived. Next-door neighbor told us we wouldn't have got much out of him, anyway. He needed twenty-four hour care to take a shit. So really, she did him a favor."

"Husband?" repeated the principal with a squeak. "She never mentioned anything about a husband."

"Yip," said Royce, "seems like no one knew about him. He really should have been in a home for vegetables, but she had him on some kind of ventilator to keep him breathing. No telling how long he'd been in a coma. She'd been cashing in his war pension checks for years."

Principal Harvey looked at the man in horror. It was clearly news to him.

"Thank you for your time, Principal Harvey," said

Sergeant Harry. "If we need anything else, we'll be in touch."

"I'll be in my office if you need me."

Principal Harvey stamped out his cigarette, pirouetted on his heels and stormed off in a huff. As he reached the end of the corridor, he burst into tears again.

"Strange little man," said Harry, shaking his head.

The policemen exchanged a puzzled look and went back inside the classroom.

We peered up at the policemen from our books.

"Now, kids. Don't mind us," said Harry. "We're just having a look around. We'll be in and out."

Royce opened up Milden's desk drawers, and lifted out a pair of lace women's underwear, handcuffs, and the girdle. He tried to be discreet about it, but failed miserably.

"Strange," said Royce. "Have a look in the cupboard back there, Harry."

Harry walked past rows of desks with twenty-eight pairs of eyes tracking his every move. Peter stepped out in front of Harry and attempted to block his path.

"We checked it already," said Peter.

Harry pushed the boy out of the way, but he scampered in front of him again. "She's not in there."

"Of course she's not in there, kid," said the sergeant. "We're looking for evidence."

Harry picked the child up and dropped him back onto his seat. He muttered to himself, "Strange kids." He opened the cupboard and took a mental inventory of its contents. Nothing unusual about a dirty shovel, rubber gloves, rope, a tennis racket and hockey stick. He shut the cupboard door.

"Nothing here," announced Harry.

"Yeah, I guessed as much. Didn't think we'd find anything," said Royce.

The floorboards creaked as Royce walked away from Milden's desk. He rocked back and forth on the same spot, causing the loose floorboards to squeak even louder. I'm sure we were all equally terrified.

Had we not secured the floorboards properly?

My body went cold with fear.

What if the police officer tried to lift them and found the grave?

"They really should get these floorboards nailed down firmly," said Royce. "Harry, was there a hammer in that cupboard?"

"Maybe," said Harry.

He went back to the cupboard and scratched around. Unsurprisingly, there was a hammer lurking in one of the corners. "She's almost got the entire garden shed in there."

He walked up to Royce and passed him the hammer. Royce pounded down each of the loose nails, firmly securing the floorboards. He stood up and rocked back and forth...that time, not so much as a creak.

"That's better," said Royce.

The policemen gave each other a nod for a job well done, and headed for the door. Without a single fidget or blink, we watched the two men walk out. We could still hear their voices echoing as they walked down the hallway.

"Well-behaved kids," said Royce.

"No shit, they're like robots," said Harry.

"She must have been one hell of a teacher."

Harry gagged. "No man, she was a fucking cunt."

I wonder if there was a story behind Harry's words. Maybe he grew up in this sleepy hollow we called home? And if he did, then maybe...just maybe...once upon a time, Ms. Milden was his teacher too.

CHAPTER 10

J acob's eyes were closed and he had a wide smile on his face. Jordan had no idea that his grandfather had such a fertile imagination.

Jordan sniggered to himself. He'd never heard of a teacher so mean, so cruel, so inhumane, so deserving of her orchestrated fate. He wanted to know more backstory. How long had the kids been planning it? Who came up with the nefarious plot in the first place? He hoped Gramps wouldn't portray himself as being the mastermind in the story. The plot may have been ingenious, but it was very fucked up, and rather disturbing.

Did Jacob construct this elaborate tale simply to distract both of them during his final hours? Jordan couldn't figure it out. Everything was described in such exquisite detail.

Some parts were so convincing they could almost be...true.

Almost...but surely not.

He knew he shouldn't believe a single word. How could he possibly trust the ramblings of an old man high on death-quickening doses of morphine? The story was ludicrous, from start to finish, none of it made any sense. What sane person would believe that a class of eight-year-olds could possibly put such a macabre plan in motion, let alone come up with it in the first place?

But the tale was still chilling. The depth and detail of his grandfather's words made the story sound all too real.

He entertained the thought, *what if it were true*, however improbable? It would make Jacob part of one of the most twisted acts of retribution ever committed. But the fact that his grandfather implicated himself was reason enough not to trust a word of it. Jordan would have been more inclined to believe the story if it had come from someone else, or starred a different cast of characters that didn't include his grandfather. Jacob was such a passive old man, who always sat quietly in his armchair reading a paperback, who never raised his voice or got angry about anything, not even line jumpers. He most certainly wasn't the killing kind.

"Come on, Gramps," said Jordan. "Do you really think I'm going to believe that you murdered your teacher?"

Jacob never replied, though his smile grew even wider still.

"Gramps?"

The heart monitor stopped beeping and the EKG reading flatlined. There was no struggle.

The old man drifted away peacefully.

Jordan held his grandfather's hand and kissed the delicate wrinkled skin. A tear ran down his cheek.

"Goodbye, Gramps."

Rebecca skidded into the room, and saw that the end had finally come for Jacob. Her face was a mix of relief and sadness. She went to his side and switched off the heart monitor, ending the shrill monotone cry of the machine.

"I'm sorry for your loss," said Rebecca.

"Thank you," he replied. But he didn't want to lose his grandfather now, or say goodbye.

"It was good to see him so happy, so lucid in his final hours," said Rebecca.

She lay a hand on Jacob's shoulder and gave the old man a smile. "He looks peaceful lying here."

Jordan shot her a quizzical look. He had no idea what she was talking about.

"Did you know my grandfather?"

"I did. Though I haven't seen him in many years."

Jordan stared at the nurse and said nothing.

Rebecca continued, "I used to work as a psychiatric nurse. Jacob was a patient of mine once."

"What?" said Jordan, startled. "Why would he need to be admitted to a psychiatric hospital?" His tone was defiant.

Rebecca tilted her head to one side and squinted at the confused young man. "You really don't know?"

Jordan shook his head. He felt his blood pressure rising, and his breathing quickened.

Rebecca sighed, and took a moment to choose her words carefully.

"From what I remember, the doctors weren't certain of the diagnosis, but he was having a psychotic episode. He had a terrible delusion that the police were coming to take him away. He was terrified. He was an inpatient for a few weeks, and then I never saw him again...until now."

Jordan thought back to the brief discussion between the doctor and nurse about Jacob's medications. The drug he was taking, risperidone, he remembered what it was—an antipsychotic.

But there was nothing wrong with his grandfather's mental health. If it were true, then someone in the family would have known about it. A secret like that doesn't stay hidden for an entire lifetime.

But it had to be true.

The nurse had no reason to lie to Jordan.

He was mortified.

"The stories he told me," continued Rebecca. "I never met anyone who could confabulate the way he did."

"You mean make things up?"

"Oh yes," she said with wide eyes. "He should have been a writer."

Jordan stared at the nurse, his feelings alternating between shock and denial.

"Are you sure?" he asked, his voice trembling.

Rebecca gave him a gentle nod and a look of pity.

"I had no idea. I don't think anyone in our family knew." He looked down at his grandfather's body and shook his head. "Jesus, Gramps. What other secrets have you been living with all these years?"

"I apologize. I shouldn't have said anything."

"It's okay. If you hadn't, I guess I'd never have known." He buried his face in his hands. "I just can't believe it."

"My condolences for your loss. He was a good man," said Rebecca, before she left the room.

Jordan felt an overwhelming sadness for the old man. Had his grandfather suffered alone all these years? Did no one else in his family know, or were the grandchildren shielded from the knowledge by their parents, to protect their innocent and untainted view of the sweet old man?

He wished he could go back in time and do something to help Jacob. He wasn't sure what exactly, but if he'd known about his grandfather's mental health issues he could have at least been there to support him through any times of difficulty. But it was too late now. There was no point reflecting on it and going over endless what-ifs. Jacob was gone, and there was nothing that Jordan would ever be able to do to change what had happened in the past.

He held Jacob's hand. The room felt quiet, too

quiet, now that the machines were no longer blipping and beeping.

After a few minutes, the silence was broken as a stream of family members flooded the room.

"Is he...?" cried Jordan's aunt, June.

"He's gone," he replied, confirming their worst fears.

And so the tears began to flow.

Jordan quietly extricated himself from the hospital room.

He found himself standing outside the main hospital entrance, his walk through the hospital had been in a complete daze. The skies had turned grey and the first drops of rain were starting to fall. Trevor pulled up in their battered old Nissan. Jordan climbed into the passenger seat. Trevor tried to form a smile, but one look at Jordan's bloodshot eyes told the whole story. Trevor held him in the tightest, loving embrace as Jordan sobbed on his shoulder.

"He's gone to a better place now. It's okay, babe."

It took a few minutes for Jordan to calm down before they drove away from the hospital. He stared out the window at the pouring rain, trying to make sense of the thousand thoughts he had running through his head.

"If you need to talk about it...?" said Trevor, reaching for Jordan's hand.

"No...I'm okay."

He gave Trevor's hand a squeeze to add credence to his words.

CHAPTER 11

J ordan realized that all he'd accomplished in the last hour was shifting piles of shit from one side of the study into neat piles on the other side. It was soul-destroying and back-breaking work. His eyes swept across the room to judge the state of it. What he saw only made him more depressed than he already was.

He decided he needed a break from the seemingly insurmountable task of packing up the study, and instead assigned himself the simpler goal of clearing out the main hallway closet under the stairs. Jordan figured he could at least get this small space finished before dinner time.

He and Trevor only had until the weekend to get as much sorted as possible before his mom and dad would take over, and the two young men planned to drive back home. His parents were stressed enough as

it was, that the more the two young men could accomplish, the better.

The floorboards in the closet creaked and groaned
under Jordan's feet. He took an armful of clothes that
were hanging on the racks, and threw them into large
black trash bags.

The dust that erupted from the mishmash of
decades-old suits, jackets, and even some of his long
departed granny's dresses, kicked his allergies into
overdrive. His eyes were watering and his nose itching
like crazy within a few short minutes. The itching
worsened until he erupted into a sneezing fit that
went on for five minutes straight.

When he finally got the sneezing under control,
he picked up an extraordinarily heavy box of crap and
started lugging it into the hallway.

Jordan's foot caught on something hard and
metallic attached to the floorboards. The box went
flying, and crumpled as it hit the floor, spreading its
contents of old shellac 78 jazz records everywhere,
shattering a few in the fall.

Jordan sustained a rather nasty bump to the head.
He lay on the ground, nursing his swollen temple,
half expecting that Trevor would come rushing to his
aid, but his boyfriend was missing in action, obviously too engrossed in whatever he was doing in the
kitchen to register the loud crash in the background.

Jordan fished around on the floor of the closet and
discovered something peculiar. There was a trap door
hidden beneath the mountain of shoes and scattered

clothes. He had to pull out another stack of clothes to fully expose the trap door, and found that it was latched shut and locked with a rusty padlock.

He scanned the area for something he could use to prise open the lock, but came up empty handed. He raced back into the kitchen and saw Trevor staring at the news on the television.

"Babe, you should stop and watch this," said Trevor, pointing at the television, but Jordan was on a mission and didn't pay attention to a word coming out of Trevor's mouth.

He grabbed the toolbox that was sitting on the kitchen counter and ran back down the hallway to the storage closet. He unclipped the toolbox and found a sturdy looking screwdriver, which he slipped through the loop of the padlock and used all the force he could leverage. The padlock remained tightly shut, but the bolts around the latch began to come loose.

Jordan tried again, heaving with all his might. The bolts flew off and the latch broke into several pieces. Jordan toppled backwards, and smacked his head on the floor.

"Ouch!" he said, nursing the back of his head. "Fuck that hurt."

Jordan got up and tried to open the trap door again, but it was jammed shut. He put himself into a squatting position over the handle and heaved till he was blue in the face. One final, almighty haul, and the trap door swung open.

Jordan stared down at a rickety wooden ladder that disappeared into the darkness below.

A little voice inside his head was telling him not to climb down... that people don't put locks on doors they want opened... that nothing good would ever come of finding out what lay beneath, but curiosity got the better of him, and he took the first step.

He slowly lowered himself into the darkness where there appeared to be a basement below the house. Jordan gagged on the musty stale air. The pungent smell of mold and damp made it hard to breathe, and he lifted up the end of his shirt to cover his mouth and act as an air filter. He could hear Trevor calling out for him from the kitchen, but he was too preoccupied with his new discovery to respond.

His eyes began to adjust to the dark and he was able to just make out the outline of a switch on the nearby wall. He reached out and felt a light switch, which he flipped to turn on. A solitary light attached to the centre of the ceiling slowly illuminated. Only a wan light at first, but growing brighter by the second, revealing the basement and its chilling contents.

The color drained from Jordan's face.

He couldn't make sense of what his eyes were seeing.

"What the fuck is this, Gramps?" he uttered to himself.

From the thick layer of dust that covered every surface, he guessed that nobody had been down here in a very long time; years or maybe even decades. The bare brick walls were covered with maps of the city and district, and an orgy of mottled photographs, faded "Missing Person" newspaper clippings, and red lines criss crossing and connecting them to one another. Some of the photos had big red crosses through their faces; others were circled with notes scrawled beneath.

Jordan was terrified, and didn't want to take another step closer, but he knew he had to. There were dates on the clippings, and ages of the people in the photographs spread over several decades. The most recent newspaper clipping, was a story about a man in his early fifties with severe dementia who had disappeared from a rest home across town.

At the very centre of the disturbing collage was a faded monochrome photograph of a class, a pretty young female teacher standing in the centre, surrounded by her pupils. The kids in the front row were smiling sweetly and holding a small chalkboard that read "*Classroom 1-D - Miss Milden*".

Jordan recognized one of the children's faces. He double-checked the list of student names printed below the photo to be sure. It was definitely his grandfather, although unlike he'd ever seen him before. The way the camera captured his eyes, they seemed to stare right into Jordan's soul.

Ms. Milden wasn't an old witch.

She was young... beautiful.

He turned around and his blood ran ice cold. The

floor had been dug up and dirt was piled in one corner. There was a pit in the floor. Jordan stepped gingerly forward until he could see over the edge. The light hanging from the ceiling barely illuminated the floor, and he could see nothing but blackness in the pit below.

How far down did it go?

Jordan took his mobile phone out of his pocket and switched on the LED light. He swung the beam of light across the pit and froze.

There were skeletons half buried in the dirt. Skulls, rib cages and long bones protruding.

Urine flowed down Jordan's thigh and collected in his shoe.

He turned and looked back at the photographs, the maps... red rusted saws, nail gun, grinder and other tools sitting on the shelves.

Not tools... implements of torture.

Jordan stumbled backwards and scrambled up the old ladder, breaking the first rung. He lost his footing and landed his chin on the rung in front of him, biting down hard on his tongue. He spat blood onto the floor and clutched his mouth in pain.

Taking a deep breath, he climbed up the ladder, more carefully this time.

Trevor crashed into Jordan as he stepped out of the closet and into the hallway.

"Don't ignore me," growled Trevor. "I've been calling for you."

"I'm sorry, I—" but he was cut off mid-sentence.

"You're not going to believe what they found in the old school grounds. It wasn't just the one body. They found human remains from at least eight different victims, some murdered decades apart. They think there might be more, so they're bringing in a special forensics team."

Jordan became lightheaded and queasy, but fought off the dizziness with a few deep breaths.

"What's wrong?" asked Trevor.

"Nothing. I'm not really feeling myself today."

Trevor gave him a hug. "It's been a tough week, hasn't it?"

He lay his head on Trevor's shoulder and soaked up the affection. "What else did the news say?"

"They think they've identified one of the bodies already."

"They have?" Jordan straightened himself up.

"Yeah. In the seventies, one of the teachers from Ridgemont Elementary went missing. She was walking home from school one evening, and was never seen again. They matched some teeth that they found with old dental records."

"Did they give her name?"

"Miss Mildew, or something like that—"

"Milden?"

"That's the one. How did you know?"

"I must have heard it somewhere before."

Jordan whimpered, and his hands began to shake. His heart was a void, as if his soul had been ripped from his body. He understood now. Everything was starting to make sense. The story his grandfather told him, it was a confession of sorts, a confused, muddled version of events—a disturbed mind's version of the truth.

Jordan stared blankly at the floor beneath his feet.

Trevor looked him dead in the eyes and tapped his forehead. "What's going on in there?"

Jordan's face crumpled and his eyes welled with tears. He held onto Trevor and cried his heart out.

"It's okay, babe" said Trevor, rubbing Jordan's back and comforting him. "I know you miss him. It'll be okay."

Trevor glanced at the closet and saw nothing but a jumbled mess, just as it had been when they first arrived at the house. He closed his eyes and rested his head on Jordan's shoulder.

"It's all going to be okay."

The End

ABOUT THE AUTHOR

The eldest of the brothers. Warren was born in England, where he spent his childhood terrorizing his younger brothers on his parents' livestock farm. The family cashed up and emigrated to the United States when he was a teenager. After high school, he worked in the IT sector until the crash in the early 2000s when he decided to head back to University to study English and French, with the dream of becoming an author.

www.warrenbarns.com
warren@thebarnsbrothers.com

Printed in Great Britain
by Amazon